Tilda Teaches

Chatterboxes

To Toby and Rafi, my five boisterous children and the biggest chatterboxes I know
–AA

Made with love by the team at

FIVE MILE

Tash, Niki, Jade, James, Lena, Andy, Amy, Amanda & Caity

Five Mile,
the publishing division
of Regency Media
www.fivemile.com.au

First published 2020

A catalogue record for this book is available from the National Library of Australia

Printed in Australia by Ovato 5 4 3 2 1

Tilda Teaches Chatterboxes

FIVE MILE

PENCILS
SURF
STICKERS

Chapter One

Hi, I'm Tilda. Here are three things you need to know about me.

1. My favourite colours are green and sparkles.
2. When I grow up I'm going to be the World's Best Teacher.
3. I have just been on the most amazing holiday ever.

Every summer holidays I go camping with my TEAM, Harry and Binky.

They are my **T**otally **E**xcellent **A**wesome **M**ates. We all live on the same block. And they are in my grade at school.

Sure, we are best friends forever. But Harry, Binky and I are more than BFFs. They're my TEAM. Get it?

My TEAM and our families always have epic camping adventures. We've been camping together since we were tiny kids.

Back then, we had little-kid sleeping bags with fairies and dinosaurs on them. Now the TEAM have proper grown-up sleeping bags with cool patterns and stripes on them. And we're allowed to sit close to the campfire.

And we get to toast our own marshmallows. Epic, right?

But this summer I didn't go camping with my TEAM.

Mum and Dad took Baby Joe and me on a different summer holiday this year.

Instead of packing my backpack and sleeping bag, I packed my suitcase and a new roly-poly bag with a pull-up handle to take on the plane. That's right. I got to go on an aeroplane! Twice. There and back.

And I got to roll my roly-poly bag right up to my seat on the plane. I had packed books and pens and teddies inside. And some notepads and stickers and stamps. And a sleeping mask. And some secret chewing gum that Mum didn't know about.

But I ended up just looking out my little aeroplane window the whole time.

What a view!

Both times, the plane landed before I even opened my roly-poly bag!

Mum, Dad, Baby Joe and I flew to the top of the country. That's where my cousins Coco and Ivy live.

Coco and Ivy are the coolest! They are way older than me. Ivy has lost twelve teeth.

And Coco is allowed to walk to the shops. All by herself!

I hung out with Coco and Ivy for two whole weeks. So brilliant!

We went to trampoline parks and scary rollercoaster parks and waterslide parks and wildlife parks. Coco and Ivy live in a fun-park paradise! And every day I ate coconut ice-cream.

Yumlicious! That's right, it was *yummy* and *delicious*! Even better than toasted marshmallows.

My TEAM may have had their own epic camping adventure. But I just know that my summer holiday was way more exciting.

Who wants squashy tents and rinsing sandy clothes in the shower every night?

Tomorrow I will see Harry and Binky at school.

I can't wait to tell them about my amazing holiday.

They are going to be super jealous when they hear about it. For absolute sure.

Chapter Two

I just love the first day of a new school year. Don't you?

You get to meet your new teachers and see your new classroom. And you find out what days you will have sport and music and, most importantly, art.

But this first day back at school, I'm most excited about seeing Harry and Binky. I haven't seen them in **longever**. You know. So *long* that it feels like *forever*.

I have bubbles of excitement fizzing up inside me as I run through the school gate. I race into the schoolyard at top speed. And then I spot my TEAM. They are at the monkey bars.

Harry is wearing his purple cap with the lion on it. He only wears that one on special days. Like the first day back at school.

Binky's frizz-mop of hair is bigger than ever. You can probably see it from space.

I'm so puffed out when I get to the monkey bars that I can't talk. But my TEAM are so happy to see me.

TILDA

'Tilda!' cheers Binky. 'I missed you so much. Camping just wasn't the same without you.'

'Yeah totally,' says Harry. 'We had nobody to show us how to make a mandala with leaves and pebbles. Or how to build a sandcastle that doesn't get washed away by the waves.'

I can't help smiling.

'Aw, I missed you guys too!' I puff. 'But I had the *best* time with Coco and Ivy. Wait until you hear all the stuff we did.'

'Us too!' says Binky. 'The TEAM – minus you, Tilda – had the most epic camping adventure ever. We even made a campfire treat that's better than toasted marshmallows ... Chocolate chip damper!'

Wow! That does sound yumlicious! Maybe even better than coconut ice-cream ...

'And you won't believe it when we tell you about the flood,' Harry says, swinging across the monkey bars. 'Binky's dad's sleeping bag was so deep underwater that he had to sleep with a snorkel!' Harry snort-laughs and swings upside-down.

'Yeah,' says Binky. 'In the morning Mum blocked the end of the snorkel. Dad woke up honking like a goose. It was so funny!'

OK, that does sound funny. I laugh, but it sticks in my throat. My laugh comes out as a frog croak.

The school bell rings and Harry drops like a monkey from the monkey bars.

I walk with my TEAM to our new classroom.

'Well, I have to tell you about my holiday,' I say. 'I hung out with Coco and Ivy the whole time. We went on six different waterslides!'

I talk faster as we walk down the hallway. 'And we made up a cool trampoline dance. I did a flip and ended up on Coco's shoulders!'

'That sounds like our First Ever Family Camping Talent Show,' says Binky.

Harry laughs. 'Yeah, it does.'

'What's that?' I ask.

'Oh, just something new we started,' says Binky. 'For our act Harry carried me in on his shoulders. It was a bit scary at first, but then we did this giant robot routine.

It was so funny. And then we ...'

I'm not really listening to Binky anymore. My tummy is starting to feel a bit weird.

We walk into our new classroom. For the first time ever I don't feel like looking around at all the new things in the room. I slump into a chair behind one of the desks instead.

TILDA

Harry and Binky sit behind me. But I don't turn around. I play with the zip on my new pencilcase.

What's going on? My TEAM should be talking about my brilliant holiday. Not their boring old camping trip.

The weird feeling is growing in my tummy. And it's not the first-day-back-at-school excitement bubbles.

Chapter Three

The weird feeling stayed stuck in my tummy all day.

It was there during art class. It was there when I played Peekaboo with Baby Joe after school. And it was there at night-time too.

It was even there when Mum and Dad did their 'We're Having Tacos For Dinner' dance. And tacos are my most favourite food.

The weird tummy feeling is still in there now. Even after two **yumlicious** tacos.

I wonder. Could it be my heart, not my tummy that is being weird? I have an idea about how to find out.

My new teacher Miss Emmanuel (just about the nicest teacher ever!) gave us a worksheet today called 'I See, I Hear, I Feel'.

She asked us to use the worksheet to help sort out our thoughts before writing.

It really worked.

It was really easy to write about my holiday after I filled in 'I See, I Hear, I Feel'.

Three gold stars to Miss Emmanuel for her excellent worksheet!

My thinking needs some sorting out! I could really use that worksheet right now.

So I get up from my bed and sit down at my desk.

I open my Teacher Tilda notebook to a fresh page. Then I draw three bubbles.

I use my neatest writing to write the headings and then I write under each one.

I HEAR

- Harry and Binky laughing at their funny memories of the camping trip.
- Harry and Binky talking all day about the super fun things they did together.

I SEE

- The four perfect shells Harry found at the camping beach for my shell collection.
- The kookaburra feather that Binky brought me.
- All the cool stuff I brought back from my holiday, that Harry and Binky won't be interested in.

I FEEL

- Jealous of how much fun they had without me.
- Disappointed that I didn't get to tell them about my holiday.

So that's it! I'm *jealous* and *disappointed*. I'm **jealoppointed.**

That's the weird feeling in my tummy. And it is not a nice feeling at all.

But I can't help it.

What if Binky and Harry keep talking about their camping trip forever?

That thought is so terrible that I flop my head down on to my desk.

CRUNCH! I flopped onto something crinkly and crumply.

Oh no! Not my crinkly, crumply, crafty, creative chatterboxes! I quickly push them all back into shape.

My cousins showed me how to fold paper chatterboxes on my holiday. And what I learned was that playing chatterboxes is fantastic fun!

I start to feel that little fizzle in my fingers. The one that I call the **teaching tingles.**

Yes! I will teach Binky and Harry to make chatterboxes! That will help them forget all about their camping trip.

And maybe they will let me tell them about my holiday.

I write a plan in my Teacher Tilda notebook.

Step 1:
Teach my TEAM how to play chatterboxes.

It's easy, but there are lots of different ways to play. So I had better teach them all the ways to play first.

Step 2:
Let the chatterbox-making begin!

The weird feeling in my tummy has gone. Now my insides feel warm and fuzzy. I am sure my TEAM will be so busy with Chatterbox Class, they will forget everything else.

Binky and Harry will be like 'Camping trip? What camping trip?'

Practice at
word
Acrostic poem

Chapter Four

I find it hard to listen in class on Tuesday morning.

I know Miss Emmanuel is giving us gold-star tips about how to study for our spelling test. But I can only think about lunchtime. Why isn't it lunchtime yet?

When the lunch bell finally rings, I grab my little bag of chatterboxes. Harry and Binky follow me to our spot under the giant tree.

'Woah, Tilda. What's going on?' Harry asks, jogging to keep up with me.

I sit down under the tree. That's when I see that Harry is wearing his 'smart kid' cap today. It says '$E=MC^2$'

on the front. I have no idea what that means.

But I do think a 'smart kid' cap is the perfect hat to wear when you're about to learn something new.

'Welcome to Chatterbox Class,' I say. I use my best Teacher Tilda voice.

Harry and Binky look at each other.

'What?' says Binky. 'I mean, Tilda, I know you talk a lot. But why do you need to teach us to be chatterboxes too?'

'No, no. Not that kind of chatterbox,' I say, laughing. 'This kind!'

I tip my little bag upside-down. The colourful paper chatterboxes rain down on to the grass.

‘Cool, origami!’ says Harry. He picks up a chatterbox and turns it over.

‘Well, it is a bit like origami,’ I say. ‘But these are not just for looking at. They’re for playing with! Look, I’ll show you how they work.’

I pick up my bright purple chatterbox. I hook it over my fingers. Each corner has a number written on it.

‘Pick a number, Bianca,’ I tell Binky.

I choose her first because I know Binky loves numbers. And I call her Bianca when I’m teaching because that’s what teachers call her.

Binky points to the 5.

I open and close the chatterbox five times with my fingers.

When I finish, the chatterbox is open like a tiny bowl.

Inside it says the names of four animals.

'Pick an animal,' I tell Harry.

He points to 'cheetah'. Of course. Cheetahs are Harry's favourite animal. Because they are super speedy like him.

'C-H-E-E-T-A-H' I spell out. I open and close the chatterbox with my fingers as I spell.

When I finish, there are fruits written inside the tiny bowl. Binky points to KIWI.

Carefully, I lift up the flap that Binky chose.

Under the flap the writing says, 'You are a superstar! Do six star jumps!'

Binky isn't very sporty, but her star jumps are perfect.

A second later Harry is shouting 'My turn!'

I teach them how to play with all my different chatterboxes for the rest of lunchtime.

One chatterbox tells Harry to be an angry dinosaur. He is so good at it! Binky and I fall sideways laughing.

Another chatterbox tells Binky to spin around seven times. She is so dizzy, she crashes into the tree.

Then a pink chatterbox tells Harry to share his funniest holiday memory ever.

Urgh! I forgot that was written in there. I wrote it in the first chatterbox I ever made with Coco and Ivy. But it is too late now.

You have to do what the chatterbox tells you. That's the rule!

Harry scrunches up his forehead, thinking hard.

I am hoping Harry will say a holiday memory that all the TEAM have shared.

'Got it!' he says. 'Binky, how about when the seagull stole a chip out of your hand?'

'Yeah,' says Binky. 'But the chip was so heavy that he dropped it in Mum's milkshake!'

Harry snort-laughs.

I am not feeling great. My class was supposed to make Harry and Binky forget about their camping trip!

Luckily the end-of-lunch bell rings.

'OK, class,' I tell them in my clearest Teacher Tilda voice. 'Tomorrow I'll teach you how to fold your very own chatterboxes. Excellent work today everyone.'

Teachers always need to be encouraging. Even if what they're teaching is super-duper easy.

Chapter Five

On Wednesday I'm busting to get down to the big tree at lunchtime.

I've brought my very special coloured pencils and some squares of fancy coloured paper.

It is so important that chatterbox paper is square.

It just won't work if you start with a rectangle. Believe me, I've tried it. A total **messaster**. You guessed it. A *messy disaster*. A big one.

My TEAM arrive at the big tree as I am setting out the class materials on the grass.

Harry's wearing a four-leaf clover cap for good luck. Binky's holding a ruler.

'What's the ruler for?' I ask.

Binky looks worried. 'Won't I need it to check my folding? I'd hate to make a mistake.'

'Don't worry, Bianca. I promise it's really easy,' I say.

I use my calming Teacher Tilda voice.

'Now, everyone take a piece of paper. I'll teach you how to make chatterboxes. Step by step.'

I use 'hands-on teaching' in my Chatterbox Class. Mum told me that 'hands-on teaching' is when your students do something with their hands in class.

It's much more fun than just listening to or watching the teacher. And it's easier to learn if you're having fun!

Have I told you yet that my mum is a primary school teacher? And my dad is a history teacher? They don't teach at my school. But it is handy to have parents who are teachers if you are going to be the World's Best Teacher when you grow up.

Don't you think?

I show the class the green square of paper I have chosen for my chatterbox. Binky picks orange. Harry finds a bright yellow one at the bottom of the pile of coloured paper.

I show them how to fold the corners. All the points meet in the middle, making an X-shape with the four flaps.

‘Now we flip our paper over and do that again,’ I say. ‘Next it’s time to write inside your chatterbox.’

I show my students where to write. On both sides of the chatterbox. And under each of the flaps.

I cup my hand over my pen. 'Always hide your writing. So we surprise each other when we play.'

Soon the chatterboxes are finished. It's time for me to teach everyone how to use them.

'We fold them in half and squeeze our fingers under the flaps.' I say.

Binky goes first. Her chatterbox is filled with number puzzles! There are some really tricky math problems inside.

Binky's chatterbox tells us to work out what three quarters of 24 is.

Harry and I have to work together to find the answer. And it totally wears my brain out!

Harry's chatterbox looks cool. It is decorated with colours and animals on the outside. But under the flaps are some really tough challenges.

Harry's chatterbox tells Binky to sprint to the monkey bars and back.

Harry's chatterbox tells me to do 19 push-ups. It wears my body out!

My arms feel like spaghetti when I'm finished!

It's my turn. I've made a super cool fortune-teller chatterbox. I have a mystery answer under each flap.

'Ask my chatterbox a question and it will tell you the future. Like magic!' I say.

'Will I ace tomorrow's spelling test?' Binky asks.

She points to a flap and bites her lip as I lift it up.

Absolutely is the answer under the flap.

Binky looks so happy!

It's Harry turn to ask my chatterbox about his future.

'Will I get a world record for Most Amazing Chatterbox?' he asks.

Harry is so desperate to get a world record.

But when I lift the flap it says *Hmmm ... Not sure!*

The end-of-lunchtime bell rings.

I realise that we have had a whole lunchtime without a single word about camping.

Three gold stars for Chatterbox Class!

Chapter Six

At lunchtime on Thursday I lay out all my coloured paper in a big rainbow. That way my students will see all the colours at once.

Being prepared is an important part of being a teacher.

'Welcome Chatterbox Champions!' I say when Harry and Binky arrive.

(See how encouraging I am? I probably deserve a gold star for that.)

'Today we'll be playing Choose Your Own Cheery Chatterboxes,' I say. It took me ages to think up this game. But I just know that my class are going to love it!

'Not more chatterboxes!' Harry groans. 'We've been doing this all week.'

'He's right,' says Binky.

I can't believe it.

'No offence, Tilda,' says Harry. 'It's been fun. But can we find something else to do with this paper?'

'Paper planes?' says Binky.

'Yes!' cheers Harry.

'Oh Harry, how fun was that amazing paper plane competition we had on the camping trip?' says Binky.

'Yeah, that was so cool!' Harry agrees.

'Let's do that,' says Binky. 'But we'll have to make sure our planes stay inside the playground. We don't want to get in trouble for going out of bounds.'

Paper planes are the last thing I feel like making. Firstly, because I don't want to hear about their holiday.

And, secondly, because I've tried making them before. Secretly, I'm not very good at it.

But I know that Binky and Harry are right. We have been playing with chatterboxes a lot.

So I decide to give their idea a go. I take a piece of silver paper and fold it here and there.

I'm not sure what I'm doing.

Binky and Harry are folding like crazy and talking to each other.

'Remember that giant glider your dad folded?'

'It went so far!'

I feel like Binky and Harry have forgotten I'm even here.

'Yeah, and how funny was it when your jet plane got stuck in the tree?'

'It's probably still there now!'

'Yeah, or that kookaburra has made it into a nest.'

'The one that kept squawking every morning! So noisy!'

Binky's and Harry's paper planes look perfect. And they fly perfectly too! Soon their planes are zooming across the school oval.

Binky and Harry are throwing and catching and laughing.

My plane looks wonky and floppy. It flies for two seconds and then drops into the mud.

I give it a couple more goes. But it's just not working.

Binky and Harry are far away by now. In the middle of the oval with their perfect planes.

I don't think they have noticed how grumpy I am. In fact, I feel like they don't notice me at all.

Chapter Seven

Friday is usually my absolute favourite day at school.

And not because it's almost the weekend.

It's because every week, that's when we do our Show and Share talks.

Today is our very first Show and Share for the year.

Miss Emmanuel asks who would like to start.

Harry and Binky shoot their hands up before me.

Miss Emmanuel explains to everyone that she chooses Harry and Binky because they raised their hands nicely and didn't call out.

Gold-star teaching, Miss Emmanuel!

Teachers must always encourage good manners in their students.

Binky and Harry go up the front together to share. You guessed it. Their camping holiday.

Harry talks about the epic flying fox at the campsite.

Binky talks about the amazing rocks they saw on their hike. She holds up a little fossil pebble that she found in a cave.

Harry reaches his fingers right up to the ceiling. He's showing how big the waves were that he body-surfed on the beach.

Binky talks about the type of jellyfish that stung her.

READ
TILDA

She even shows everyone the red mark on her leg that is still healing.

Everyone's eyes are glued on Harry and Binky. Even Miss Emmanuel's.

Everyone is going 'ooh!' and 'aah!' at the right moments.

I think this is the best Show and Share anyone has ever seen.

I was planning to Show and Share about my holiday too.

But now I have that weird tummy feeling again. I must be **jealoppointed.**

But what can I do? There's no way I can run Chatterbox Class to fix my weird tummy feelings this time.

I need a new plan to make the weirdness go away.

I can only think of one other thing to try. I'm going to have to tell my friends how I'm feeling.

Mum always says that when you have something tricky to say, just stick it in a sandwich.

Sounds crazy, right?

It's true. My mum can be pretty crazy at times.

But what she means is this.

First you say something nice. That's the bread. Then you say the tricky bit. That's the sandwich filling. Then you say something nice again. That's the other slice of bread.

Mum says that the tricky hard bit won't sound so bad if you say the nice things too.

At lunchtime Harry, Binky and I are sitting under the big tree.

It's time to try the sandwich idea.

'Guys, I'm so happy that you had such a great time on your camping trip,' I say. 'It sounds like you did so many cool things.'

That's my first slice of bread.

I take a really deep breath for the next bit. The hardest part.

'But you've been talking about it so much. It makes me feel a bit jealous that I wasn't there. And like you're not really interested in hearing about my holiday.'

My heart is beating really fast. But I have finished the tricky bit!

'Also, your Show and Share talk was totally perfect. An excellent mix of interesting and scary and hilarious and science-y!'

And that was my other slice of bread.

Phew! I take a deep breath.

For the first time since I started talking I look up at my friends' faces.

Binky looks so sad. Like she might cry.

'Oh no!' she says. 'Tilda, I'm so sorry! I didn't know you felt like that. You should have told us earlier.'

'I guess we have been talking about our camping trip a lot,' says Harry. 'And you're right, we haven't asked you about your holiday.'

'So let's fix that right now,' says Binky.

My weird tummy feels OK again.

'Yeah,' says Harry. 'We want to hear every detail.'

'Ready, set, go!' they say together.

Chapter Eight

By Friday night I feel like I've been down the biggest waterslide 33 times.

Totally zonked!

My fingers are covered in paper cuts from so much chatterbox folding.

My voice is croaky from telling Harry and Binky everything about my holiday.

And my brain is worn out from all the time I spent trying to work out how to stop feeling **jealoppointed.** Luckily my tummy is now feeling totally un-weird!

I have one last thing to do before I start my weekend.

It's time for my Weekly Report. Writing student reports is a very important teacher job! So I practise every week.

It's pretty fun because I get to think about everything that happened during the week. The good stuff and the not-so-good stuff.

In my very best teacher writing, I begin.

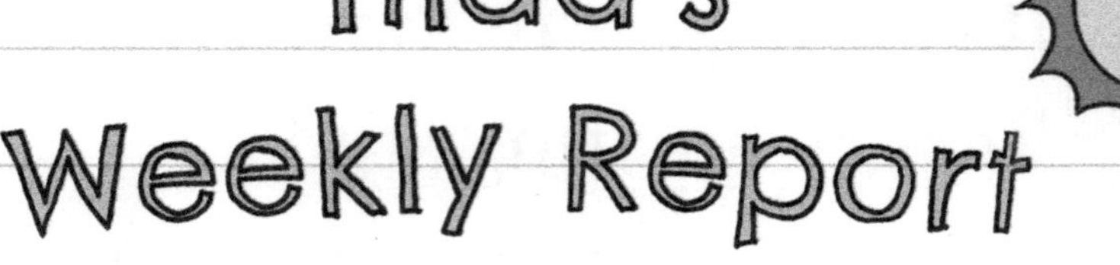

Tilda's Weekly Report

Teaching: A+

This week Tilda taught her friends how to make chatterboxes. Brilliant teaching of course!

Being a good friend: B

Tilda wasn't very cheery for her friends when they talked about their holiday memories. Tilda needs to work on sharing in her friends' happy stories.

Communication: A

Tilda did an excellent job of telling her friends how she felt, using a perfect sandwich. Next time, she should try to tell them even sooner.

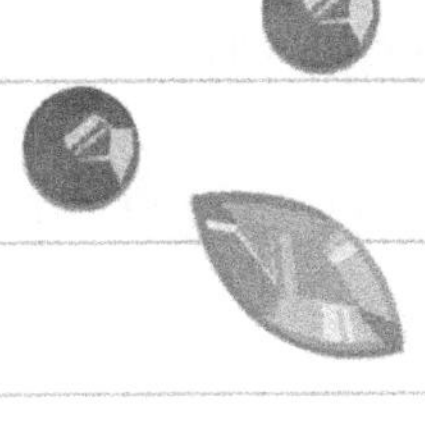

Wow. Now I'm not just feeling zonked. I'm feeling pretty proud too.

It wasn't much fun hearing about all the stuff Harry and Binky did without me. But I did have my amazing holiday with Coco and Ivy.

Next summer we'll have another TEAM epic camping adventure together. And we'll make new memories.

Hopefully without a giant flood.

And now we've got a year to plan our act for the Second Ever Family Camping Talent Show!

I grab my fortune-teller chatterbox from my desk.

I ask it 'Will Harry and Binky forgive me for being a bit of a grump this week?'

I carefully unfold the flap and read what it says underneath. *Definitely!* I think this chatterbox is almost as smart as Binky!

So I ask it just one more question.

'Is Teacher Tilda going to be the World's Best Teacher?'

I hold my breath as I unfold the flap to read what it says.

7
8
1
2

For Absolute Sure!

I flop back on my bed, close my zonked eyes, and fall fast asleep.

THE END

Some behind-the-scenes moments from the story you just read ...

One of my fun holiday snaps at the water park!

Dad made a monster taco on taco night!

I practised making paper planes, and look how good I got!

MAKE YOUR OWN CHATTERBOX

You'll need square paper and pens.

2. Flip over and fold again

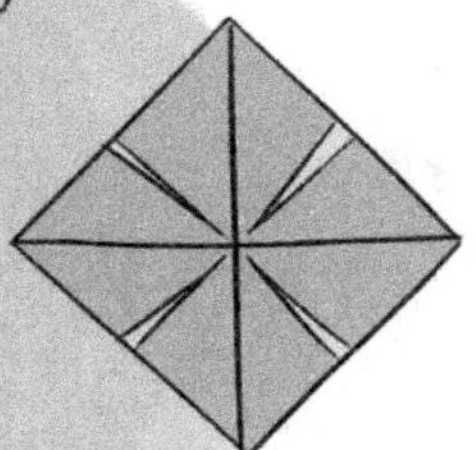

3. Draw on each side (and inside the flaps)

Time to play!

Read more Tilda

Tilda can't wait to show Binky and Harry what a superstar swimmer she is, with her splashy splashes and fishy flips! But when she realises she can't swim properly, Tilda is **embuzzled**. That's right, embarrassed and puzzled! Maybe Tilda will feel better if she teaches her friends something actually cool – like cartwheeling! Tilda's Cartwheel Class is super fun, until it rolls out of control ...